MEET ALL THESE FRIENDS IN
BUZZ BOOKS:

Thomas the Tank Engine
The Animals of Farthing Wood
Biker Mice From Mars
James Bond Junior
Fireman Sam
Joshua Jones
Rupert
Babar

First published in Great Britain 1994 by Buzz Books,
an imprint of Reed Children's Books
Michelin House, 81 Fulham Road, London SW3 6RB
and Auckland, Melbourne, Singapore and Toronto

The Animals of Farthing Wood © copyright 1979 Colin Dann
Storylines © copyright 1992 European Broadcasting Union
Text © copyright 1994 Reed International Books Limited
Illustrations © copyright 1994 Reed International Books Limited
Based on the novels by Colin Dann and the animation series
produced by Telemagination and La Fabrique for the BBC
and the European Broadcasting Union.
All rights reserved.

ISBN 1 85591 392 5

Printed in Italy by Olivotto

Spring
Awakening

Story by Colin Dann
Text by Mary Risk
Illustrations by The County Studio

The winter had been long and hard for the
Farthing Wood animals. But now at last,
spring was arriving at White Deer Park.

A stone near the pond wobbled and a long
body wriggled out from under it. Adder was
coming out of hibernation.

"Ah, the sssun!" she said. "Sssplendid!"

Toad had crawled out of his hole too.

"Got to go home, mateys!" he croaked.
"Got to get back to Farthing Wood!"

"Thisss isss your home now," said Adder.

But strong instincts were pulling Toad towards the place of his birth. He began to hop towards the boundary fence.

Vixen was teaching her cubs to hunt. Fox kept watch, in case of danger.

"They're fine cubs, Fox. You must be very proud of them," said Badger.

Vixen pushed a fir cone in front of the cubs' fumbling paws.

"Now, pounce on it!" she told them.

Bold rushed forward. He grabbed the cone and tossed it in the air.

One of the cubs had wandered off to play.

"Come back, Dreamer!" called Vixen. "Pay attention! You must learn to hunt."

"It's easy!" said Friendly. "Watch me!"

"Show off!" yapped Bold, and he gave his brother a nip.

Charmer licked Friendly affectionately.

"Bold didn't mean to hurt you," she said.

Fox went off to hunt and Badger fell asleep.
Suddenly Vixen sniffed the air. A big blue
vixen stepped out of the bushes.

"My my," she sneered. "What fine cubs!
A pity they're such a common, nasty colour."

"Keep away from them!" snapped Vixen.

"My dear," drawled Lady Blue, "I've got
better things to do with my time."

Bold rushed at Lady Blue. She snarled, and sent him flying with a flick of her paw.

"Teach him to behave himself," she said. "Scarface doesn't like cheeky cubs."

Lady Blue stalked off. Vixen licked her cub.

"Dear Bold," she said. "Thank you for trying to help, but you're too young to fight."

Bold was soon distracted by something else.

"Stop, Bold!" called Vixen. "It's Mole, and my goodness, he's got some babies!"

"I'm not Mole," said the stranger. "I'm Mateless. Mole was my mate, but he died."

"Mole dead?" cried Vixen. "Oh no!"

She looked at Badger, who was still asleep.

"These are Mole's babies," said Mateless.

Just then, Badger opened his eyes.

"Badger," said Vixen. "Meet Mole's mate."

"Moley? About time too, my friend," said Badger. "Where have you been?"

"No, Badger, this is Mole's mate and his babies. I'm afraid Mole has died," said Vixen.

"Nonsense!" said Badger. "He's just hiding."

Vixen was quiet. They'd all miss Mole.

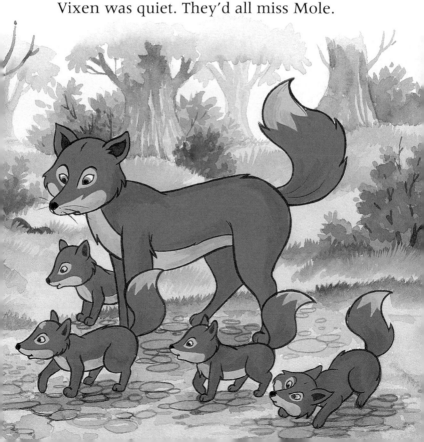

Adder was worried about Toad.

"The sssilly creature hasss gone back to Farthing Wood," she hissed. "Doesssn't he remember? We left the Wood becaussse thossse dreadful humansss had invaded with their bulldozersss."

As Adder approached Fox's earth, the cubs spotted her. Bold picked her up playfully and tossed her in the air.

"Bold! Stop that!" barked Fox. "Adder's a friend!"

"Sorry Adder," said Fox. "He won't do that again, I promise you."

"Says who?" said Bold cheekily.

Fox ignored him. "How are you, Adder? How are the other animals at the pond?"

"Toad isss misssing," said Adder. "Hisss homing inssstinctsss are taking him back to Farthing Wood."

Toad had already left White Deer Park behind. The countryside passed in a kind of dream as he hopped along in a daze.

"Got to get home! Got to get back to Farthing Wood!" he muttered to himself.

He didn't notice the stream he was passing, or the boy who was fishing in it. He didn't notice the other toad, either.

But the boy did.

"Gotcha!" he said, scooping up the other
toad with his grubby hand.

Quickly, he dropped her in a jam jar and
screwed down the lid. He put the jar down
and looked round.

"There's another!" he exclaimed.

Before Toad knew what was happening,
he was in a jar too, with the lid firmly shut.

17

Whistler and Kestrel had come to look for Toad. From up in the sky they saw it all.

"Kee! He's in the glass thing!" called Kestrel.

"There are two toads," said Whistler. "Which one is ours?"

"Let's fly down and take a closer look," Kestrel suggested.

The boy was tired of walking. He wanted to paddle in the stream. He put his jars down next to each other and took off his shoes and socks.

Toad looked through the glass, and there, in the other jam jar, he saw Paddock.

"She's beautiful!" thought Toad.

He closed his eyes, then opened them again to make sure he wasn't dreaming. She was still there. He smiled.

"Oh! He's handsome!" thought Paddock.

She smiled back at him.

Whistler dived down, picked up the string of a jar in his beak and flew off with it.

"Hey! Stop, thief!" shouted the boy.

"That's not Toad in that jar!" called Kestrel. "You've got the wrong one!"

Whistler opened his mouth to speak, and accidentally dropped the jar. It fell to the ground and smashed.

Paddock sat among the broken glass, stunned. Then she gave herself a shake.

"No bones broken," she said. She looked up at Whistler. "Thanks, heron!" she called, hopping away.

"Kee! There's nothing for it," Kestrel told Whistler. "You'll have to go down again and get the other jar."

Toad was still stuck in his jar. He leaned back against the glass.

"She was so lovely," he thought. "But where's she gone?"

Suddenly, his whole world turned upside down. He was being carried into the air! He looked at the ground. It seemed miles away. He shut his eyes in terror. The jar swayed from side to side.

"Crikey!" he moaned, turning greener than ever.

Gently, Whistler set the jar down outside
Fox's earth. The Farthing Wood animals
crowded round to look at Toad.

"Are you all right, Toad?" said Vixen.

"He can't hear us in there," said Fox.

Toad looked up. Faces swam above him.

"Is that you, Fox?" he croaked.

"We must get him out of there," said Vixen.

"Easier said than done," sniffed Owl.

"I could pick him up and drop him," said Whistler hopefully. "It worked before."

"I don't think you should try that again," said Fox. "It's too dangerous. Only a human can deal with this human thing. Whistler, take Toad to the warden!"

The warden's cat was sunning herself on the doorstep. She looked up in astonishment as a heron landed beside her with a jam jar dangling from his beak.

"What are you doing?" she asked.

"Toad's stuck in the jar," said Whistler. "We need the warden. Can you fetch him, Cat? Please?"

Cat yawned and stretched.

"I might," she said, "and I might not. What do you want the toad for? Are you going to have him for dinner?"

"Certainly not! He's my friend!" said Whistler indignantly.

"You must be one of the Farthing Wood lot," yawned Cat. "All right. I'll help."

She lifted her head and miaowed loudly.

The warden came to the door.

"What's this?" he said, and opened the jam jar.

Toad hopped out. He looked dazed.

"Quick, Toad!" said Whistler.

Toad jumped onto Whistler's beak.

"Well, I never!" said the warden, as Whistler flew off with Toad.

Toad's friends were relieved to see him.

"Toad, are you all right?"

"Say something, Toad!"

Toad stood up and began to hop away.

"He's trying to get back to Farthing Wood!" said Badger. "We must stop him!"

"Got to find my sweetheart!" said Toad.

Suddenly, he smiled with delight. Paddock had arrived.

"Will you come to the pond with me?" she asked, smiling at him shyly.

Toad eagerly followed his new mate.

"I do believe Toad will be staying at White Deer Park after all!" said Fox, grinning.